Pete Likes Bunny

Emily Arnold McCully

Holiday House / New York

Copyright © 2017 by Emily Arnold McCully
All Rights Reserved
HOLIDAY HOUSE is registered in the U.S. Patent and Trademark Office.
Printed and Bound in April 2016 at Tien Wah Press, Johor Bahru, Johor, Malaysia.
The artwork was created with pen and ink and watercolor.
www.holidayhouse.com
First Edition
1 3 5 7 9 10 8 6 4 2

Library of Congress Cataloging-in-Publication Data
Names: McCully, Emily Arnold, author, illustrator.
Title: Pete likes Bunny / Emily Arnold McCully.
Description: First edition. | New York : Holiday House, [2016] | Series: I
like to read | Summary: "Pete likes Bunny, the new girl in his class; and
despite teasing from classmates, Bunny likes Pete too"— Provided by publisher.
Identifiers: LCCN 2015041858 | ISBN 9780823436538 (hardcover)
Subjects: | CYAC: Pigs—Fiction. | Rabbits—Fiction. | Friendship—Fiction.
Classification: LCC PZ7.M478415 Pd 2015 | DDC [E]—dc23 LC record available
at http://lccn.loc.gov/2015041858

ISBN 9780823436873 (paperback)

For Liza and Annie

On Monday Ms. Pooch says,
"Class, we have a new student.
This is Bunny."

"Hi, Bunny," says the class.

Pete stares at Bunny.
He cannot help it.

Bunny is perfect!

Pete thinks about Bunny
all the time.

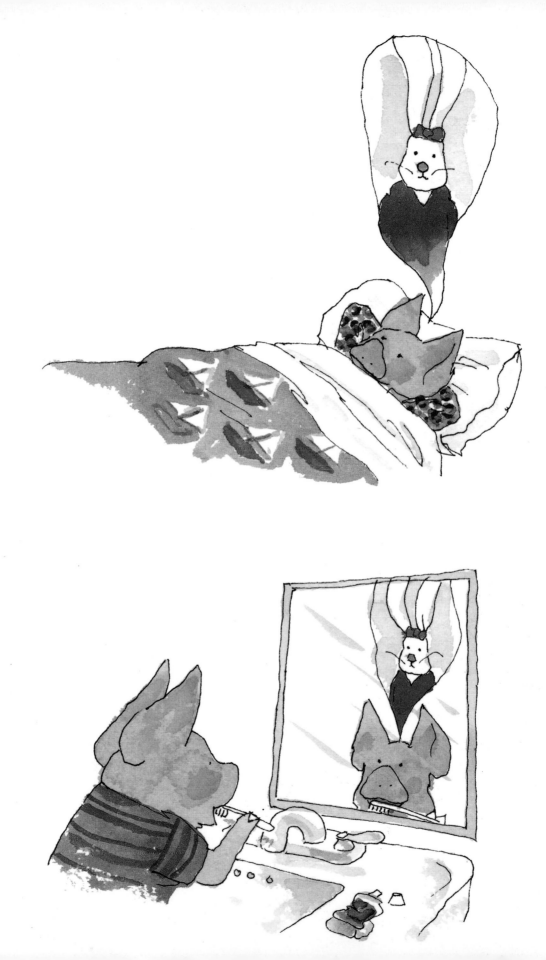

On Tuesday Pete gets on the bus.
The seat next to Bunny is empty.

Pete sits down.

"Pete likes Bunny!"

"Pete likes Bunny!"
the kids sing.

"Pete likes Bunny!

Pete likes Bunny!"

"Quiet down, class!" says Ms. Pooch.

Pete feels bad.

"Bunny will never
like me now!" he says.

Mom says, "Take her some flowers."

Pete picks a big bunch of wildflowers.

What if Bunny won't take the flowers?
He has to try. . . .

"Hi, Bunny. These are for you,"
Pete says on Wednesday.

"Hi, Pete. I made some
cookies for you,"
says Bunny.

"Bunny likes Pete!" the class sings.
"And Pete likes Bunny!"

Pete and Bunny don't mind
now because it is true.

More I Like to Read® Books
by Emily Arnold McCully

3, 2, 1, Go!

★ "McCully nails a common childhood scenario: a twosome
is playing school and won't let a third play."
Kirkus Reviews (starred review)

"This succeeds both as entertainment and instruction;
the pachyderms' social interactions and STEM
content are a delightful bonus."
Booklist

Late Nate in a Race

A BANK STREET COLLEGE BEST CHILDREN'S BOOK OF THE YEAR

Little Ducks Go

"It would be easy to believe that the energetic pen-and-
watercolor illustrations were sketched from life."
Kirkus Reviews

Pete Won't Eat

★ "New readers will eat this up."
Kirkus Reviews (starred review)

★ "The illustrations are priceless."
School Library Journal (starred review)

Pete Makes a Mistake

"This spot-on title is perfect for brand new readers."
School Library Journal

Sam and the Big Kids

"Young kids . . . will relate to Sam's story, cheer
Sam's heroism, and delight in their own achievement
of reading this title all by themselves."
The Bulletin of the Center for Children's Books

Some More I Like to Read® Books in Paperback

The Big Fib by Tim Hamilton

Boy, Bird, and Dog by David McPhail

The Cowboy by Hildegard Müller

Dinosaurs Don't, Dinosaurs Do by Steve Björkman

The End of the Rainbow by Liza Donnelly

Fish Had a Wish by Michael Garland

Good Night, Knight by Betsy Lewin

Grace by Kate Parkinson

The Lion and the Mice by Rebecca Emberley and Ed Emberley

Look Out, Mouse! by Steve Björkman

Lost Dog by Michael Garland

Moe Is Best by Richard Torrey

A Night at the Zoo by Kathy Caple

Pants for Chuck by Pat Schories

Pete Likes Bunny by Emily Arnold McCully

Pete Makes a Mistake by Emily Arnold McCully

Pete Won't Eat by Emily Arnold McCully

Sam and the Big Kids by Emily Arnold McCully

See Me Run by Paul Meisel
A THEODOR SEUSS GEISEL AWARD HONOR BOOK

3, 2, 1, Go! by Emily Arnold McCully

Visit http://www.holidayhouse.com/I-Like-to-Read/ for more about I Like to Read® books, including flash cards, reproducibles and the complete list of titles.